MW00814704

Ryan Dempster was named Special Assistant to President Theo Epstein and General Manager Jed Hoyer on December 5, 2014 after retiring from baseball as a member of the Cubs organization. In his new role with the organization, he will spend time with the club during spring training, visit the club's minor league affiliates during the season, evaluate amateur players leading up to the draft, and perform professional scouting assignments.

Ryan completed his big league career with a 132-133 record with 87 saves and a 4.35 ERA in 579 appearances, including 351 starts with the Marlins (1998-2002), Reds (2002-03), Cubs (2004-12), Rangers (2012), and Red Sox (2013). He spent nine seasons with the Cubs from 2004-2012 and posted 67 wins and 87 saves, the only pitcher in club history with more than 50 wins and 50 saves. He was named an All-Star in 2008 with the team, a season that marked his return to the rotation in which he went 17-6 with a 2.96 ERA to help the Cubs to their second-straight N.L. Central division title.

A native of British Columbia, Ryan retires as a two-time All-Star and a World Series Champion with the Boston Red Sox in 2013, his final season in the majors.

www.mascotbooks.com

For more information, please contact:
Mascot Books
560 Herndon Parkway #120
Herndon, VA 20170
info@mascotbooks.com

CPSIA Code: PRT0515A
ISBN-13: 978-1-63177-063-0

Printed in the United States

CLARK THE CUB
AND HIS
JOURNEY THROUGH TIME

Ryan Dempster

Illustrated by Danny Moore

Clark, the official mascot of the Chicago Cubs, was busy getting ready for another baseball game. He was proud of the Cubs and proud of Wrigley Field, the team's ballpark.

Just like the Chicago Cubs players, Clark prepared for each game by running the bases, taking practice swings in the batting cage, and fielding ground balls. Clark practiced new cheers and thought of new ways to support his favorite team.

After his pre-game workout, Clark was exhausted! Fortunately, there was time to rest before the start of the game.

As Clark was making his way back to the clubhouse, something unusual caught his attention. It was a note tacked to the ivy-covered outfield wall at Wrigley Field. The note read:

Dear Clark,

    Your great-grandbear, Joa, is proud of you for becoming the new Chicago Cubs mascot. He said that every good mascot needs to know the history of the team and field that they represent, so take this gift.

–Your friends at the Lincoln Park Zoo

Suddenly, Clark noticed a baseball appear on the ground. It wasn't like all the other baseballs at the park. There was something different about this ball…it was glowing!

"Well, that's funny," said Clark laughing to himself. "I definitely thought I put all of these away. He picked up the baseball, still carrying the note in his other paw. He looked at the two items and smiled at the thought of Great-Grandbear Joa, the first Chicago Cubs mascot. But then he shrugged, knowing there was still work to do before the game.

He decided to get in one last practice swing with the baseball he found. Grabbing a bat and jogging toward home plate, Clark tossed the glowing baseball into the air and swung as hard as he could. He watched the ball fly over the left field wall, over the bleachers, and land on Waveland Avenue. A home run!

"Yes!" he said, pumping his fist in the air as he rounded the bases and touched home plate. He felt like he'd just scored a game-winning run in the bottom of the ninth inning of the seventh game of the World Series. As Clark crossed home plate, the ball magically appeared in his paw. Shocked, Clark smiled, tossed the ball in the air, and caught it. Then, something amazing happened.

Bright colors swirled around him, and he felt the ground fall from underneath his feet. Wrigley Field was transforming right before his eyes! *What's happening?* he wondered.

When everything settled again, Clark saw construction workers working under a sign that read "Weeghman Park".

"Where's Wrigley Field?" he wondered aloud.

"I don't know!" said a voice beside him. He looked around and saw Joa floating next to him.

"Grandbear! What are you doing here? Where am I?" asked the little cub.

"Well, I wanted to show you Wrigley Field in my day. Or as we called it, Weeghman Park," said Joa.

"Wait, you mean we're in the past?" asked Clark with wide eyes. He looked around in wonder at the construction.

"Yes, indeed!" replied Joa.

Cubs Fact!

October 3, 1915: Cubs play their last game at West Side Grounds, beating St. Louis 7-2.

"COOL!" shouted Clark. "Hey, but what year is it?" he asked, stopping in his tracks to scratch his head. But before he could think too long, someone interrupted his thoughts.

"Hey there – you wanna give us a hand here?" someone called out to Clark.

"Who, me?" asked Clark getting excited. "Sure!" He ran over and asked, "Say, what year is it anyway?"

"It's 1914, and we're building Weeghman Park," said Clark's new friend.

"Weeghman Park? But where's Wrigley Field?" asked the cub with a frown on his face.

"Wrigley Field?" asked the man, squinting his eyes. "Never heard of that. This place here belongs to Charles Weeghman. He owns the Chicago Federals."

"Oh," said Clark, trying to hide his surprise. He didn't know who the Chicago Federals were, but he knew they weren't the Cubs.

"But cheer up, kid. It's still baseball!" said his new friend.

With that, Clark smiled again and finished helping out with the construction. Afterwards, he thought he should move on so he gave the glowing ball a toss.

Cubs Fact!

At a construction cost of $250,000, a 14,000-seat ballpark was constructed in just two months. It was named Weeghman Park, later to become Wrigley Field. It consisted of a single-story grandstand that stretched from the left-field foul pole around home plate to the right-field foul pole, with a small bleacher section in right field.

When he caught the ball, the swirling colors reappeared. Clark and his magical baseball had traveled through time again! Clark now found himself in the stands of a stadium surrounded by tons of cheering fans. He looked around and decided that he wasn't in Weeghman Park anymore. But down on the field, there was someone he did recognize.

"Hey! That's my great-grandbear!" Clark said to the fans around him. He knew now that he was in Wrigley Field. His heart swelled with pride. This old field looked like the one he knew, but it was also different in many ways.

"What year is it?" he asked the fans.

"Why it's April 20, 1916! This is the first Cubs game at Wrigley Field!" said one of the fans.

Of course! The Chicago Cubs were celebrating their new mascot, Joa the Bear. His great-grandbear! He had heard this story many times from his great-grandbear, but now he was watching it. Clark watched in amazement as his great-grandbear was led around the field by the Lincoln Park zookeeper. He was much younger than when he was a ghost. He must've been right around Clark's age.

When his great-grandbear was led off the field, the umpire yelled, "Play ball!" and Pat Pieper's voice boomed through the megaphone.

But Clark knew it was time to travel again. He tossed the ball in the air, and was whisked away.

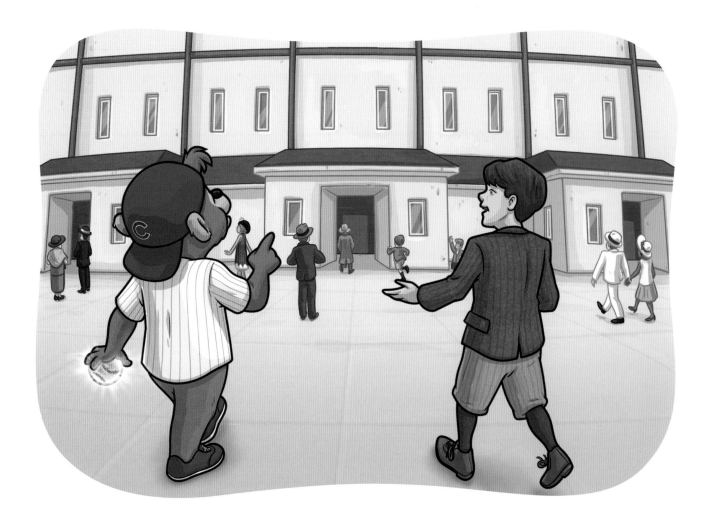

"Hey, that's the field I know!" said the bear looking up, with the magic baseball safely back in his paw.

"Ah, everyone knows Wrigley Field," said a kid walking by.

"Uh, thanks!" said the cub running to catch up. "My name's Clark. What year is it?"

"Hi, Clark, my name's Stanley and it's 1927. That's my mom over there. When she was a girl, this stadium was called Weeghman Park. It was renamed Wrigley Field after the 1926 season."

"Cool!" exclaimed Clark. "Why was it named Wrigley Field?"

"After William Wrigley, Jr., of course!" said Stanley.

"Come along now, Stanley," called his mother. "It's time for us to go in."

"See you later, Clark!" called Stanley.

Clark waved goodbye to his new friend. All of a sudden, Great-Grandbear Joa appeared next to him.

"Grandbear! I guess that's how Wrigley Field got its name. No wonder we didn't recognize the place in 1914. It was still Weeghman Park then."

Joa nodded, smiling. "Even I'm learning things on this journey with you! Give that baseball another toss!"

Clark tossed the ball and was amidst a sea of swirling colors again.

Cubs Fact!

Starting in 1916: William Wrigley, Jr. became involved with the team. He became the majority owner in late 1918.

Cubs Fact!

August 25, 1922: Cubs beat Phillies 26-23 in highest-scoring game in Major League history.

When Clark landed, his great-grandbear was still next to him. They were right in the middle of a huge crowd at Wrigley Field. "Grandbear, do you know what year it is?" Clark asked.

"It's got to be October 8, 1929, the year Wrigley hosted its first World Series game. Look at this crowd!" said his great-grandbear. "Temporary bleachers were erected over Waveland and Sheffield to accommodate all these fans. A record 51,556 fans attended this game."

Clark saw the bleachers and all the fans cheering around him. He was having the time of his life. "Who's playing?" Clark asked.

"It's the Cubs against the Philadelphia Athletics," said his great-grandbear. "Next year will be 1930 and the Cubs will draw an even bigger crowd for their game against Brooklyn!"

"I'm glad you're here to explain this to me, Grandbear!" exclaimed Clark. "Let's keep traveling!" With that, Clark threw the magic baseball up in the air again.

This time, Clark noticed that time was moving faster. When he caught the ball, he found himself right in the middle of Wrigley Field!

Suddenly, a player ran onto the field causing the crowd to cheer wildly. It was Jackie Robinson! Clark knew then that he was in the year 1947, the year Jackie Robinson made his Wrigley Field debut. He waved furiously at Jackie, and when he caught his eye, Clark gave the baseball player a thumb's up, which Jackie promptly returned. Before he tossed his magic baseball again, Clark noticed that the iconic center-field scoreboard at Wrigley Field was painted the famous dark green color that he knew, instead of the reddish-brown with a white clock he'd seen in the past.

Cubs Fact!

May 18, 1947: *Jackie Robinson made his Wrigley Field debut. It was the largest regular-season paid crowd in the park's history to that date (46,572).*

Clark was whisked away from the roaring crowd and found himself in the middle of a different type of field. It wasn't even a field, it was a court! He was in the middle of a Harlem Globetrotters game.

"Yikes," laughed Clark, and he jogged off the court and sat on a nearby bench.

"That was a close one," said one of the players seated near Clark.

"I'll say," said the little bear. "Say, I thought this was a baseball field."

"Well it is, but on August 21, 1954, Wrigley Field installed a basketball court and portable lights for games that featured the Harlem Globetrotters against George Mikan's U.S. Stars, and the House of David traveling team against the Boston Whirlwinds."

"Cool," said Clark. "Well, I'm a Cubs fan," he said proudly, adjusting his cap.

"I can see that," said the basketball player smiling. He patted Clark on the head before jumping into the game.

Cubs Fact!

In addition to baseball, the park has hosted football games for the Bears, soccer matches, political rallies, firework shows, lacrosse matches, track and field events, military drill shows, operatic concerts, boxing, and a lot more!

Clark tossed and caught the ball again and when he landed, Great-Grandbear Joa was next to him.

"What year are we in now, Grandbear?" asked Clark.

"This is the day of the longest game in Wrigley Field's history," said Joa.

"I remember you telling me stories about this game!" said Clark.

"Yes, it was August 17, 1982, a Tuesday if I remember correctly. A great day, but it sure was a long day. Look, even some of the fans look tired."

Clark looked around at the smiling, but worn faces and droopy eyes. "But did we win, Grandbear?"

"Well, it was a close one. The Dodgers beat us 2-1 in 21 innings. But that's alright. The game lasted a total of six hours and ten minutes, starting on Tuesday, and lasting through to Wednesday."

"Wow!" said Clark, thinking about how he might need to prepare for a game that could last that long. "Why did it have to last that long?"

"Well, since there were no lights on the field, the players and fans all had to go home once it got dark, and continue the game the next day during the daytime."

"I guess that makes sense. How long before they got lights?" Clark asked.

But he would soon find out.

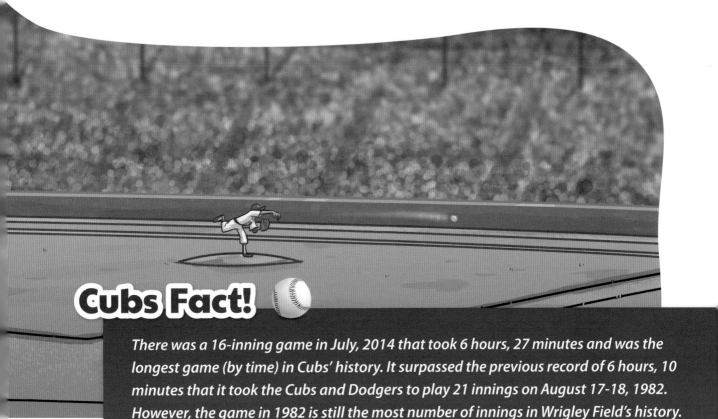

Cubs Fact!

There was a 16-inning game in July, 2014 that took 6 hours, 27 minutes and was the longest game (by time) in Cubs' history. It surpassed the previous record of 6 hours, 10 minutes that it took the Cubs and Dodgers to play 21 innings on August 17-18, 1982. However, the game in 1982 is still the most number of innings in Wrigley Field's history.

Tossing the magical baseball into the air, Clark caught it and landed in the stands of Wrigley Field once more. This time however, it was brightly-lit.

"Whoa!" said the cub. "Those lights are amazing!"

"They really are!" said a fan next to him wearing sunglasses.

Cubs Fact!

1988: *Lights were added at Wrigley Field at a cost of $5 million, ushering in an exciting new era.*

"This is great! Now the players can keep playing even when it's dark out," said the cub. He put the shades in his pocket.

"Yeah! We love it!" said the fan.

All of a sudden, Clark's great-grandbear appeared next to him again.

"Time to start hurrying along, Clark. You still have a game to get back home to and there are a few more stops to see first!"

"Oh! You're right, Grandbear," said the Cub. Clark smiled, tossed the baseball into the air, and was whisked away once more.

Clark stopped ten years into the future in the year 1998. He watched as 20-year-old Kerry Wood threw a powerful pitch toward the batter.

"I'll tell you what happened here," said Joa, appearing next to Clark. "Wood struck out 20 batters to tie a record and beat the Astros, 2-0. He allowed just one hit, an infield single. And it was just his fifth start!"

"He's a legend!" said Clark.

"He is!" agreed Joa. "This is 1998, but one more toss of the baseball should take you to 2009. See what you learn there," said Joa. Before Clark could ask questions, his great-grandbear disappeared. So he threw the magic baseball up in the air to see where it would take him next.

Cubs Fact!

In the 1990s, Mark Grace became the first Cubs player to lead a decade in hits. The first baseman also was the 1990s doubles leader and finished 2nd in singles behind the Padres Tony Gwynn.

When he landed, Clark was shocked. It was New Year's Day 2009 and Clark was in the middle of a hockey game! "Wow! Basketball games, football games, and now a hockey game! Wrigley Field has it all," said Clark.

He had landed at the National Hockey League Winter Classic. The Chicago Blackhawks were hosting the Detroit Red Wings. "This is a temperature I can tolerate!" said the bear laughing. But he knew he could not stay, so he tossed the baseball once more.

Cubs Fact!

The Tribune Co. sold the Cubs, Wrigley Field, and a 25 percent share in Comcast SportsNet Chicago to the Ricketts family, completing the deal in late October, 2009.

When he caught the ball, he was in a huge crowd in front of a stage with music blasting. Great-Grandbear Joa was next to him once more.

"Is this Wrigley Field?" asked Clark, yelling over the music.

"Yes," Joa yelled back, "it's 2013, the year *Rolling Stone* magazine named Wrigley Field the second-best rock concert venue in the whole United States."

"Woo hoo!" shouted Clark, throwing a fist into the air as Eddie Vedder, the lead vocalist for Pearl Jam, belted out the lyrics to "All the Way". Ernie Banks was right up there on stage, too. "Grandbear, do you hear THAT?" exclaimed the cub.

"Yes, I hear it all right," said Joa scrunching his nose and covering his ears. "That's young people's music," said the old bear.

Clark laughed. "Alright, let's go on home." And he tossed the baseball again.

"Wow! This looks familiar," said Clark laughing as he landed in the ballpark. "It's the year I became the Cubs mascot!" He waved hello to the fans. "Wait, if this is 2014 at Wrigley Field, and Weeghman Park was built in 1914, it must be the 100th birthday of the ballpark!" Looking around, Clark saw banners, balloons, and camera crews. He even saw the zookeeper from the Lincoln Park Zoo, who winked at Clark. Clark winked back, and then waved the baseball and note to show the zookeeper he had found them. "We're getting ready to celebrate the 100th Birthday of Wrigley Field," said Clark excitedly.

Joa appeared next to him. "You know, it's only a few minutes before game time. You better get ready!"

Cubs Fact!

During 2014, the Chicago Cubs celebrated the 100th Birthday of Wrigley Field throughout the season. Each decade was represented during ten homestands. The April 23rd game, the 100th Birthday, featured them playing the Arizona Diamondbacks in a throwback game. The Cubs wore the uniforms of the Chicago Federals, the original occupants of the stadium, and the Diamondbacks wore uniforms representing the Kansas City Packers whom the Federals played on April 23, 1914.

Clark's eyes widened. "You mean it's almost time for the first pitch?"

Joa nodded. A troubled look crossed Clark's face. He really did want to stay for the festivities, but he couldn't stand the thought of missing the first pitch.

"Can I come back here?" he asked.

"Well, I'm not sure," said Joa. "You're the first cub to time travel with a magical baseball."

"I guess you're right," said Clark. He thought for a moment, and then he knew what he had to do.

He tossed the magical baseball into the air, and ended up right back in the present. The stands were starting to fill with crowds of adoring fans. Clark reached into his pocket and saw that he still had souvenirs from his journey: the extra pair of sunglasses from the fan in 1988, his magical baseball, and the note from his friends at the zoo. But he noticed the ball wasn't glowing.

Cubs Fact!

During the 2014 season, Cubs Charities presented 100 Gifts of Service, a yearlong program that featured Cubs players, coaches, and front office associates engaging in community service projects large and small to celebrate Wrigley Field's 100th birthday. Cubs members gave these gifts of service to the community by visiting hospitals and schools, serving meals to children and families in need, renovating playgrounds, and much more.

Clark tossed the baseball into the air. He shut his eyes, waiting for the swirl of color to sweep him into a distant time, but nothing happened. Feeling grateful for what he had seen and learned, Clark smiled to himself. "Thanks, Grandbear," he said quietly.

With that, he tucked his souvenirs back into his pocket. Under the marquee he still saw decorations celebrating the 100th Birthday of Wrigley Field. It looked like the fun and games were only just about to begin!